WINDHOVER

Montem Primary School
Hornsey Road
London N7 7QT
Tel: 0171 272 6556
Fax: 0171 272 1838

To Harry and Charlotte, and Class RK (1995/6)

C.B.

To the school where the windhovers live.

A.B.

With thanks to

The National Bird of Prey Centre, Newent, Gloucestershire

Author's note: windhover is the country name given to the
kestrel because of the way it hangs on the wind.

First published in hardback in Great Britain by HarperCollins Publishers Ltd in 1997.
First published in Picture Lions in 1998
1 3 5 7 9 10 8 6 4 2
ISBN: 0 00 664613-1

Picture Lions is an imprint of the Children's Division, part of HarperCollins Publishers Ltd.
Text copyright © 1997 Alan Brown. Illustrations copyright © 1997 Christian Birmingham.
The author and illustrator assert the moral right to be identified as the author and illustrator of the work.
A CIP catalogue record for this title is available from the British Library.

Printed and bound in Singapore by Imago

WINDHOVER

Written by Alan Brown
Illustrated by Christian Birmingham

PictureLions

An Imprint of HarperCollins*Publishers*

When I open my eyes, the sky is the first thing I see, the wind is the first thing I feel. The blue sky strokes me with windy fingers, the warm sun dries my wet feathers.

I hear chipping from the egg close by
my own broken shell. A hooked
beak bursts through and gasps for air.
There is more chipping and I see a
sticky wet head. A chick struggles
out of its shell, and then another.
They are my brother and sister.

There is a sound of great beating wings and our mother flies back to the roost with food in her beak. It smells good and we screech, "Kee! Kee!" We are all hungry but I am the biggest chick and the first to be fed.

Our mother and father bring us mice and shrews as fast as they can catch them. They tear them up for us to eat and we all grow fast, but I grow fastest.

We sit out on the ledge on the edge of the sky. Soft fingers of wind ruffle our feathers and the sun warms our backs. We live in a hole the shape of a clover-leaf, high in the wall of a school. We can see across the playground and further away to the village green and the road.

We stretch our wings and beat them just like our parents. The children in the playground look up and point. "Look at the baby windhovers!" they cry. "Look at their fluffy feathers!"

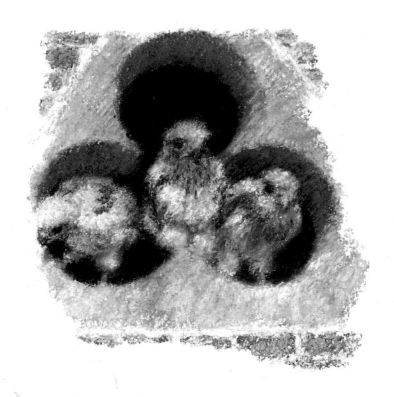

One evening after school has finished there is a sound of footsteps coming up towards us. We shuffle to the back of the roost. A dark shape looms over us and we screech, "Kee! Kee!" This is not our mother or father, this creature has no bitter bird smell. I peck at it and strike with my claws. The figure makes a strange noise and two hands hold me tight. I am bundled into darkness and taken from my home.

When the sack is opened I am dazzled by light. I try to fly but crash into strong bars and fall to the floor in a cloud of feathers. Where is my home, my parents, my brother and sister? Where is the wind and the sky? Again I throw myself against the bars and fall to the floor.

"I want you for my own, my friend, nobody else's," a voice says, but I don't understand.

I remember this boy from the playground. He is bigger than the other children and often pushes them to the ground. He never laughs or plays with them.

When he brings me food he does not tear it up and I cannot eat it. He tries to make me step on to his gloved hand but I stay huddled in the corner of the cage. I become thin and weak and long for home. I call for my parents, "Kee! Kee!"

The boy covers my head and I feel my feet being tied. I am carried where I can feel the wind's fingers in my feathers. The cover is taken off and I beat my wings and try to fly.

"Dan Foster! You stole our windhover!" A girl has seen us.

"Leave me alone," the boy shouts at her.

"What's happened to him? He's so thin!" She is brave and does not run away.

"I want to keep him," says the boy. "I want something of my own."

"A wild creature can't be your friend. You've got to put him back or he'll die," says the girl.

"I don't want him to die." The boy's voice is soft and kind.

"If you put him back I promise not to tell," says the girl.

I can hear the noise of the playground. I am nearly home!
The children crowd around us. "Windhover!" they call.
"Dan Foster has found our windhover!"

I am home! My brother and sister hiss. They
have grown bigger than me and do not seem to
know me. When I call, "Kee! Kee!" they
remember my sound and they let me in. They
walk to the ledge, beat their wings and fly out
over the playground.

The sky strokes me with its windy fingers and
ruffles my feathers. I am alone in the hole at the
top of the school.

There is the sound of great beating wings once
more! It is my mother swooping down to feed
me. She remembers her first chick and now I
know I am safe.

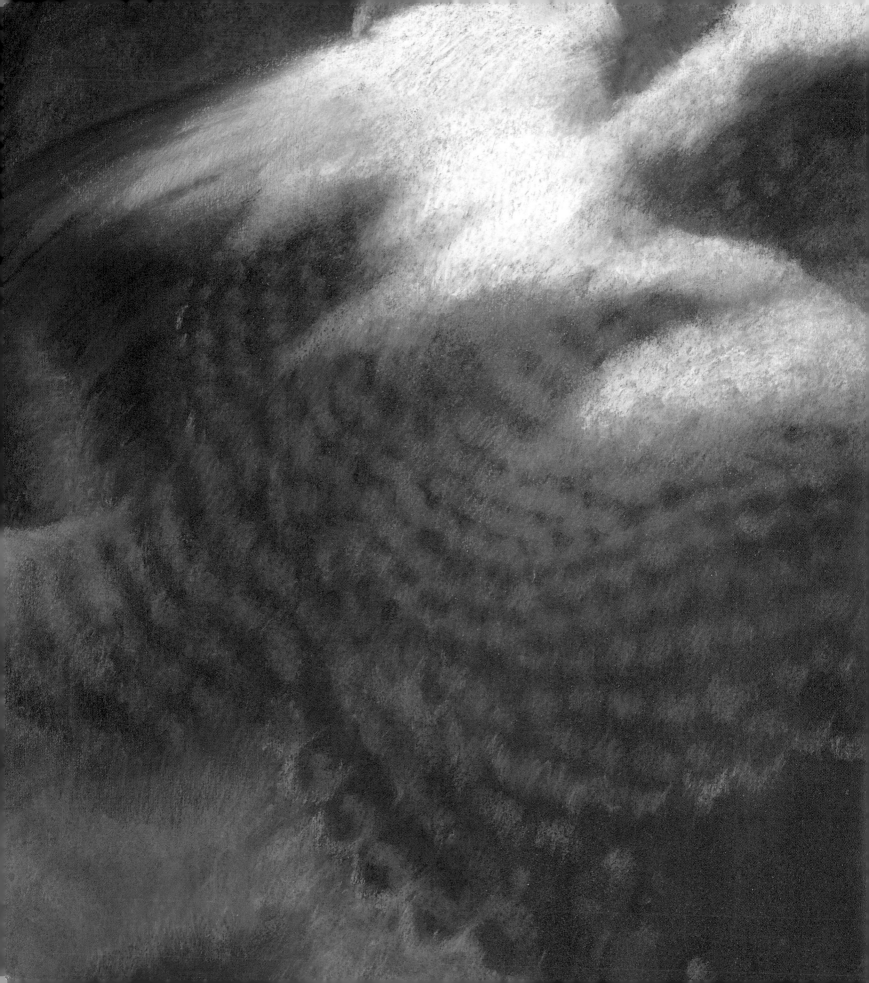

Soon my wings are smooth and strong. My fluffy feathers are gone, but I stay on the ledge at the edge of the sky. I do not want to leave home again. The children in the playground look up and call to each other, "the windhover's afraid to fly".

My father is perched on a pole across the playground. He has a shrew in his beak for me. I am hungry and call, "Kee! Kee!" but he stays on the pole.

My brother lands in a tree and calls for the food. I beat my wings. I have to fly!

Suddenly, I feel the thickness of the air and I feel the wind's fingers holding me up. I launch myself off the ledge towards the pole. I can fly! I take the shrew from my father's beak and I hear the children laugh and cheer in the playground below.

The sky and the wind are my friends. I flutter my wings to hover high in the blue sky over the school. My sharp eyes search for mice as I hover on the wind's fingers.

I see the boy with his new friend. They look up excitedly. "Windhover!" they shout. "Our Windhover!"